Sandy Creek
122 Fifth Avenue
New York, NY 10011

ISBN-13: 978-1-4351-2361-8

Printed and bound in China

1 3 5 7 9 10 8 6 4 2

The Prince & the Pauper

Once upon a time, there was a kingdom ruled over by a good and kindly king. But one day, the king fell ill and could no longer watch over his land. His son, the prince, watched anxiously by his father's bedside.

Elsewhere in the kingdom, there lived a pauper, Mickey, and his two friends—the bumbling Goofy and Pluto, his friendly dog. It just so happened that Mickey looked exactly like the prince, although he did not know it. On that particular day, Mickey and his friends were so hungry they were trying to sell fake ice creams to get money for food.

Mickey and Goofy watched as the evil captain of the guards sped by in the royal coach, which was overflowing with delicious food.

"Woof, woof," barked the hungry Pluto as he chased the coach toward the palace.

"Stop!" cried Mickey. "Come back!" He dashed after Pluto.

Pluto chased the royal coach to the gates of the palace, with Mickey right behind him. To Mickey's surprise, the royal guard bowed deeply to him and let him right through! He even called him "Your Majesty".

"Our prince is certainly dressed oddly today," thought the guard.

By now, Goofy had lost sight of Mickey and wondered where he and Pluto had got to.

Meanwhile, inside the palace, the real prince was sitting through a very boring lesson. To amuse himself, he took out his peashooter and aimed it at his servant, Donald.

"Wak!" cried Donald when he got hit.

The prince had all the food he could want and lots of fine clothes, but he often wished he could explore the world beyond the palace.

Mickey was wandering through the halls of the palace, marvelling at all the lovely things he could see.

"Look how shiny this floor is!" he said to himself. "I can see my reflection in it!"

As he walked down the hall, he thought that whoever lived here must be very lucky to have such a beautiful place to live, and so many fine things.

Mickey was so busy gazing around that he didn't see the suits of armor. He walked right into them with an almighty crash! The prince darted out of his lesson to see what all the commotion was and saw the suits of armor wobbling dangerously!

Both Mickey and the prince ended up on the floor, each hidden by a suit of armor. They peered cautiously at each other from under their helmets.

"Who could this be?" they both wondered at the same time. They were both sure they had not met before, but there was something familiar about the other one...

They both took their helmets off at the same time…and they couldn't believe their eyes!

"We look the same!" both Mickey and the prince said at once!

They examined every inch of themselves, right up to the tips of their ears. There was no doubt about it—they were identical! Then the prince had an idea…

"How happy you must be," said the prince to Mickey, "you are free to wander outside and play all day long."

"But you have lots of wonderful feasts and clothes," sighed the hungry Mickey.

"Why don't we change places for the day?" said the prince, swapping hats with Mickey. "Being a prince is easy!" Mickey thought this was an excellent idea and pretty soon they were wearing each other's clothes.

Disguised as Mickey the pauper, the prince sneaked out the window down to where the captain of the guards was stood. He waved to Mickey who was peeking out the window, wondering where on earth he would start to learn how to be a prince!

"Have fun!" said the prince.

The captain of the guards had heard there
was an intruder in the palace, and spotting
the prince dressed as Mickey, he caught him.

"That'll teach you to trespass in the palace!"
the evil guard said, as he catapulted the prince
over the wall.

"Hee, hee!" laughed the prince as he sailed
over the wall. "Even my own guard didn't
recognise me!"

The prince landed with a thump in the
snow outside the palace grounds.
"Mickey!" shouted Goofy, delighted to
see his old friend again. But Pluto, after
a quick sniff, was a little suspicious.

As Goofy swept up the prince into a great big hug, Pluto walked away slowly, convinced that this wasn't their old friend after all.

The prince, who wasn't at all sure who this strange person was, wriggled in Goofy's grip, eager to start exploring outside the palace walls.

Inside the palace, Mickey had been given an enormous speech to learn for an upcoming ball.

"Phew!" thought Mickey, "being a prince sure is hard work!" There were many royal tasks he had to do before the end of the day. He was enjoying his fine new clothes, however, and more food than he had eaten in days!

Meanwhile, the prince was learning that even though outside the palace you can wander around freely, there were some very hard things to learn—how to get food for one!

He had found some leftover chicken, but as soon as he took a bit to eat, he was immediately chased by some hungry stray dogs.

As the prince ran, he suddenly stumbled across
one of the palace guards, trying to take a chicken
away from a poor peasant woman and her children.
"Hey!" cried the prince, "Stop that at once!"

Ignoring the prince, the guard snatched the chicken and walked off laughing meanly with his friend.

"Hey," said the small child to the prince, "thank you for trying to help us, but it won't do any good. The captain and all his guards are always stealing our food."

The prince couldn't believe that the guards had been stealing food from the poor people of the kingdom!

"I have to put a stop to this!" said the prince, and ran over to the royal food wagon.

The prince flashed his royal ring at the driver of the coach. "I order you to give these people food!" the prince said.

42

A crowd gathered round the prince as he happily passed out the food that they should have had all along.

"Once I get back to the palace there are a few changes I am going to make!" the prince said smiling, as he handed round the food to his people.

Just then, the cruel guards reappeared, and saw the prince handing out the food.

"Stop right there!" the guard said, drawing his sword. The prince cowered—the guards hadn't seen the royal ring and still thought he was a pauper who was stealing their food!

Luckily, Goofy had seen everything and dashed over to the prince.

45

"Hold on!" yelled Goofy, as he pulled the prince to a passing coach. They jumped on, and managed to get safely away from the angry guards and their swords.

"Thank you so much for saving me!" said the prince as they raced away.

Later that night, as the guards feasted on their stolen food, the captain of the guards cooked up a wicked plan. He had discovered that the prince and Mickey had swapped places.

"As soon as the pauper is crowned king, I shall unmask him as an imposter and rule the kingdom myself!" he laughed evilly.

That same night, the prince found out that the king had passed away, and he was due to be crowned the next day. Although he was sad, he made a decision to be the best king he could.

Showing Goofy his ring, the prince revealed his true identity.

"I must return to the palace now and do my duty," the prince said to his new friend.

But just then, the captain and all the guards burst
into the room!

"I see your royal ring," said the captain, "but it
won't do you any good! It's the dungeon for you,
and when the pauper is about to be crowned king
tomorrow I will storm the palace to arrest him and
take control of the kingdom myself!"

The next day, a very nervous Mickey was being led to the throne to be crowned king!

"What should I do?" worried Mickey, "and where is the real prince?"

The evil captain watched from the side door, with Pluto held captive so he couldn't sniff out his true friend Mickey and give the game away.

Meanwhile, the prince had spent an uncomfortable night in the dungeon with his old servant Donald.

"Oh no!" cried the prince when they saw another scary-looking guard approaching. "How are we ever going to escape? If I don't get out in time for my coronation, our kingdom will be ruined!"

But then they noticed the guard did seem a little bumbly and clumsy. All of a sudden the new guard lost his balance and hit the other guard on the head. His mask flew off to reveal his face. It was Goofy!

"You've rescued me again!" cried the prince. Donald quacked happily.

In the throne room, Mickey was desperately trying to wriggle away from the crown.

"He's an imposter!" yelled the evil captain. "Seize him!"

"But I'm not an imposter!" a voice cried from high above. Everyone gasped when they saw the real prince swinging down to them from the ceiling!

There was a thrilling sword fight, as the prince bravely battled with the captain of the guards. Mickey watched from the throne, willing the prince on.

Just then, the chandelier that the prince had used to swing down on crashed on top of the guards, trapping them! The prince caught the evil captain's trousers on the tip of his sword.

"Eeek!" the captain squealed, and ran away, never to return! Everyone cheered.

Finally, the true prince sat down on his throne and the crown was placed on his head. He was the king at last!

Mickey and all his friends bowed deeply, happy that honor would be restored to the kingdom.

Everyone celebrated that night. Though they had enjoyed their adventures, the prince was happy to be back in his rightful place, and Mickey was just pleased to be reunited with his old pals Goofy and Pluto!

The End